Home Sweet Home, Little Kitten

By Melinda Luke
Illustrated by Darcy May

RANDOM HOUSE
Happy House Group

Text copyright © 1988 by Melinda Luke. Illustrations copyright © 1988 by Random House, Inc. All rights reserved under International and Pan-American Copyright Conventions. Published in the United States by Random House, Inc., New York, and simultaneously in Canada by Random House of Canada Limited, Toronto. ISBN: 0-394-89437-5 Manufactured in the United States of America 1 2 3 4 5 6 7 8 9 0

One spring morning, as the first rays of sunshine crept through the Millers' kitchen window, three tiny kittens were born in a wicker basket. One kitten was orange, another was gray, and the third was calico. Mother Cat looked proudly at her sleeping kittens and purred.

As the weeks passed, the kittens grew big enough to leave their basket. Soon they discovered how to chase their tails, unravel balls of string, and play hide-and-seek.

Mother Cat made certain that her kittens learned some important lessons, too. She showed them how to drink milk from a bowl and how to clean their whiskers when they were finished.

She taught them how to sharpen their claws on bark, where to hunt for food, and to stay away from unfriendly dogs. "Now you are ready to go to homes of your own," she told them when all their lessons were finished.

The very next day the Millers put a sign in their front yard. It read: FREE KITTENS TO GOOD HOMES.

Farmer Morris came from his dairy farm to see the kittens. "I'll take this little orange cat," he said. "He is just the color of my best cheddar cheese!"

Mother Cat was happy to know that her kitten would have such a nice home nearby—and a bowl of fresh dairy cream each day. The orange kitten was happy too.

FREE
KITTENS
TO GOOD HOMES

The Millers' neighbor, Mrs. Barnes, brought her daughter to see the kittens. The gray kitten climbed right up on the little girl's shoulder and purred.

"It looks as though this kitten has picked *you*!" Mrs. Barnes said to her daughter.

Mother Cat was pleased that her kitten had such a nice little girl to look after her. So was the gray kitten.

But the calico kitten was left in the Millers' yard.
"Soon I will have a home, too!" she thought happily.
The kitten waited all day, but no one came. Not that
day, or the next, or the day after that.

"No one wants me," the little kitten mewed,
blinking back a tear.

"You will find a wonderful home," purred Mother
Cat. "Just wait a little longer."

FREE
KITTENS
TO GOOD HOMES

But the calico kitten didn't want to wait. "I'll go find my own home," she decided. Just then she saw a large, friendly-looking dog walk across the lawn. "Maybe he will help me," she thought, and hurried after him.

"Meow!" the little kitten called out to the dog.
But when the dog turned to her, he didn't look
friendly anymore. He narrowed his eyes, pinned
back his ears, and bared his teeth. "Grrr!" he
snarled, and bolted toward her.
Suddenly the little kitten remembered what her
mother had taught her about unfriendly dogs!

The kitten scrambled for safety up the side of the nearest tree. The next thing she knew, she was high in the branches of the Millers' big elm. Beneath her, the dog whined and scratched at the bottom of the tree. With a yawn he finally gave up and ambled away.

"I don't know how to get down," mewed the kitten, trembling on her high branch. "Help!"

The kitten's frightened cries brought a small crowd of people to the tree.

"I'm scared," she cried loudly.

"Hold on," called the people on the ground. "Help is coming!"

Soon a shiny red truck pulled up to the curb by the tree. Moments later a ladder poked through the branches.

"Meow!" yowled the kitten as her branch swayed back and forth. Then, very gently, the kitten felt herself being lifted from the branch. A kind-looking fireman tucked her under his arm and carried her carefully down to the ground.

"You are a very lucky kitten," he said, waving good-bye.

The next day, the kitten continued her search for a home. "But I'm staying out of trees this time!" she decided. Wandering out to the sidewalk, she noticed a hole in the street. It was covered with boards, and sawhorses with flashing lights surrounded it.

The kitten peeked through the boards. But as she did she lost her balance and fell into a deep, dark pit! "Help!" she howled. "Somebody help me!"

"There's a kitten down there," shouted a voice from above. "Call the fire department!"

Soon the boards were shoved aside, and the friendly fireman's face appeared above her. "So it's you again," he chuckled. He lowered himself slowly into the hole and tucked the kitten under his arm.

"You sure are a lucky one," said the fireman.

The calico kitten purred with relief as she was lifted out of the hole.

"I'm staying out of trouble from now on," vowed the kitten the next day. She climbed to her favorite shady spot on the roof for a nap. But just as she was closing her eyes she spotted someone walking up to the Millers' house. She couldn't be sure, but it looked just like the fireman!

"Maybe I will see better from the chimney top," the kitten thought. She skittered across the roof shingles and up the chimney. But before she could see the visitor's face, a gust of wind knocked her right off her feet and into the chimney!

The kitten struggled to get a paw-hold in the chimney wall. "Phew!"she sneezed from the soot. But the more she tried to get free, the harder it was to move. "I'm stuck!" wailed the kitten.

Just then a shadow passed over the chimney opening, and a smiling face peered down at her. It was the fireman after all!

"You're lucky I saw you when I did!" said the fireman as he lifted her out. The kitten coughed and sputtered all the way back to the ground.

"I came over because I hear you are looking for a home," said the fireman. "How would you like to live with me, Lucky?" The kitten purred and rubbed against the fireman's sleeve.

The fireman talked with the Millers as Mother Cat said good-bye to her calico kitten. "You see, you *did* find a wonderful home," said Mother Cat.

When it was time to leave, the fireman gathered Lucky into his arms.

"Good-bye!" Lucky mewed as they drove away.
The ride took them past the neighbor's house where
a gray kitten lived, past the dairy farm where an
orange kitten lived...

...all the way home to where Lucky would live!
"I am lucky," she thought as she drifted off to sleep. "But not because I was rescued. I'm lucky because I found the best home in the world—mine!"